FOR TASO & LEO. —V. F.

TO MY FAMILY AND MY FRIENDS WHO SUPPORT ME THROUGH UPS AND DOWNS. —T. T.

STERLING CHILDREN'S BOOKS
New York

An Imprint of Sterling Publishing Co., Inc.
1166 Avenue of the Americas
New York, NY 10036

ISBN 978-1-4549-3381-6

Distributed in Canada by Sterling Publishing Co., Inc.
c/o Canadian Manda Group, 664 Annette Street
Toronto, Ontario M6S 2C8, Canada
Distributed in the United Kingdom by GMC Distribution Services
Castle Place, 166 High Street, Lewes, East Sussex BN7 1XU, England
Distributed in Australia by NewSouth Books
University of New South Wales, Sydney, NSW 2052, Australia

For information about custom editions, special sales, and premium and corporate purchases, please contact Sterling Special Sales at 800-805-5489 or specialsales@sterlingpublishing.com.

Manufactured in Malaysia

Lot #:
2 4 6 8 10 9 7 5 3 1
02/20

sterlingpublishing.com

Design by Julie Robine

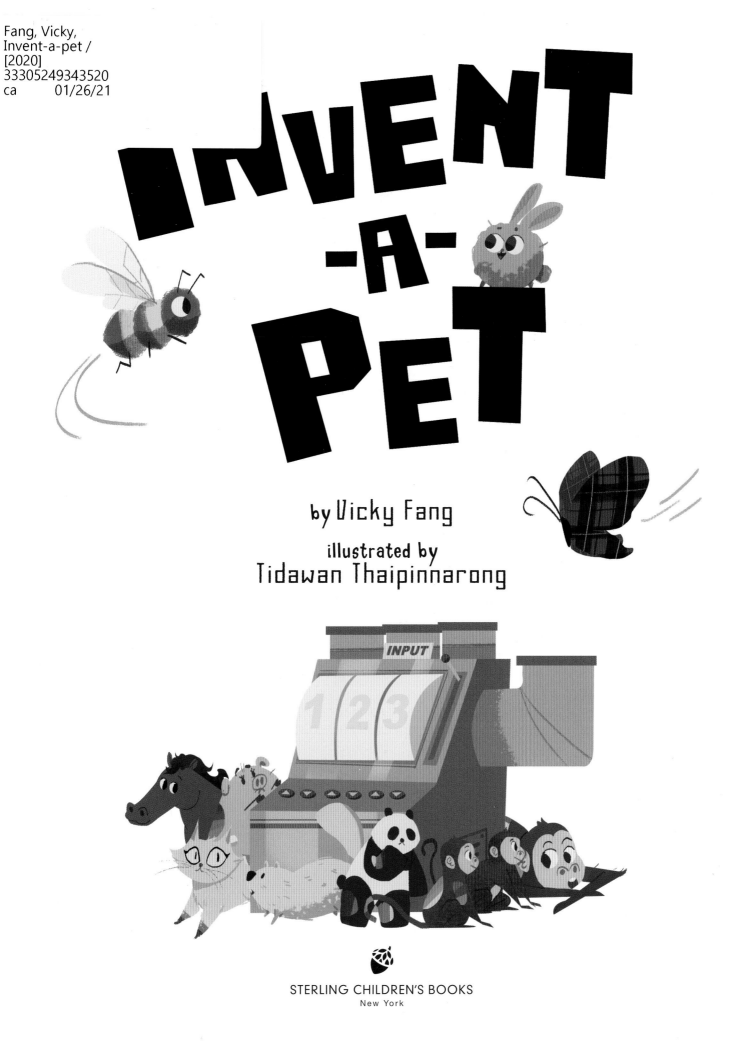

INVENT -A- PET

by Vicky Fang

illustrated by
Tidawan Thaipinnarong

STERLING CHILDREN'S BOOKS
New York

Katie was an ordinary girl who longed for an extraordinary pet.

"How about a nice goldfish?" her mom asked.

Katie refused. "A goldfish!? Too common! I need a pet that's spectacular! Unique."

One day, she came home to find a strange and magnificent machine in her living room.

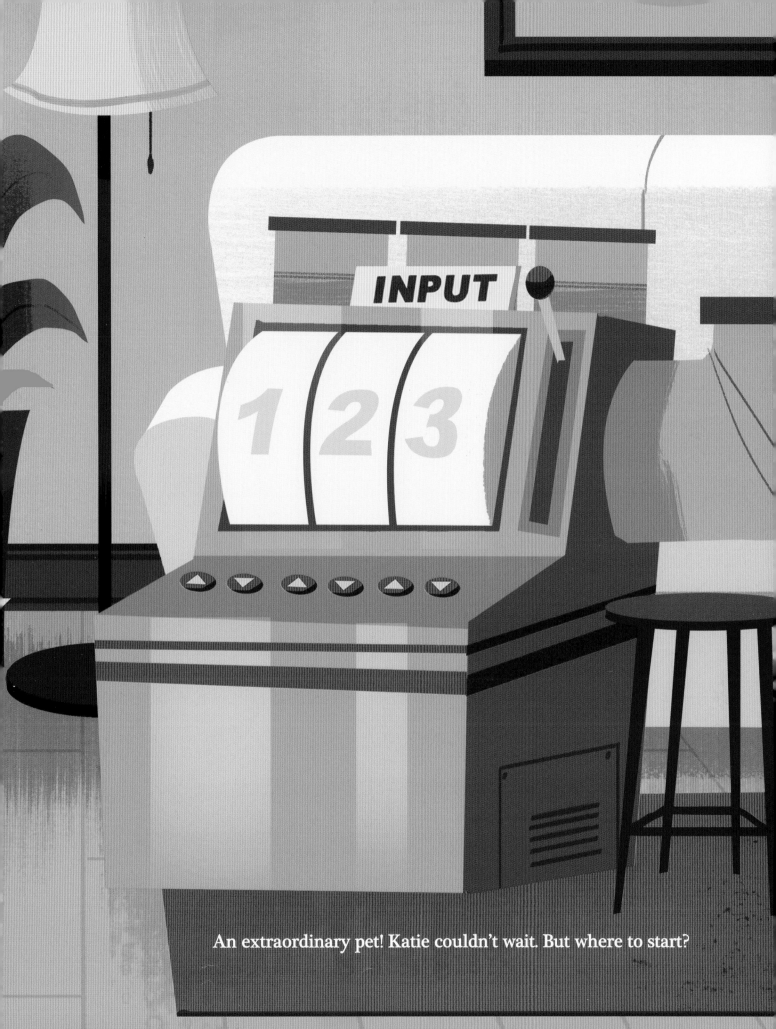

An extraordinary pet! Katie couldn't wait. But where to start?

"Hmm . . . in-put."

So, in she put . . .

A soccer ball.

A blade of grass.

A carrot.

"Unbelievable! I know just the pet to make!"

"Rainbow-colored . . ."

"With wings . . ."

"And fire-breathing!"

KA-POP!

"That's not right **AT ALL**."

"Hmm . . . flying . . ."

"Sparkly . . ."

"And beautiful!"

ZZZiNG!

"Definitely **NOT!**"

By the end of the afternoon, peculiar animals puttered, slithered, hopped, and flew about the house. None of them were right.

"How does this thing even work?"

Katie came up with a plan.

"I will figure out what each input does and find the formula for my perfect pet!"

She started with a new set of inputs. A cushion, a sock, and a banana.

"A rainbow-spotted monkey! Now, what if I just change the first item?"

Katie replaced the cushion with an armchair,
but kept the sock and the banana.

"Aha! The first item changes its **SIZE**! Now what about the second?"

Katie went back to the original items, but replaced the rainbow-spotted sock with a purple pom-pom.

INPUT

"Hmm . . . it was rainbow-spotted before, but now it's purple . . . Of course! The second item is for **COLOR**! And the third . . ."

Katie kept the first two original items but replaced the banana with a ball of yarn.

"Whoa! The third item changes the **ANIMAL**?
But how did I get a kitten?"

So Katie tried different third items.

From **SHiNY**,

to **TALL**,

to **GROSS** . . .

But the animals were never what she expected.

"I just don't understand! These animals aren't at all like the items I picked!"

She glared at her notes. And then she saw the pattern:

"Wait . . . Horses love apples, pandas love bamboo, pigs love mud. . . . The third item is something the animal loves! **THAT'S IT**, I know how the formula works!"

Before Katie had a chance to create her perfect pet, there was a great …

Luckily, Katie wasn't out of ideas. She set up an adoption center in the driveway. The neighbors were thrilled to take home her unusual creatures. In no time, the town was covered with extraordinary pets!

ADOPTION CENTER

After everyone had gone, Katie rushed to her machine. It was finally time to create *her* perfect pet. But then ... she stopped. There was one, final problem.

"Rainbows are everywhere ... wings seem so common ... What is the perfect unique pet for me now?"

Suddenly, she knew.

An apricot. A tangerine peel. A glass of water.

There it was. Her beautiful, little, tangerine-colored goldfish.

"Perfectly **EXTRAORDINARY**!"